COLOR BY NUMBER

Winky Adam

DOVER PUBLICATIONS, INC.
Mineola, New York

Bibliographical Note

Color by Number, first published by Dover Publications, Inc. in 2006, is a republication of the edition originally published in 1999.

International Standard Book Number

ISBN-13: 978-0-486-45343-9
ISBN-10: 0-486-45343-X

Manufactured in the United States by Courier Corporation
45343X05   2015
www.doverpublications.com

COLORING FUN

Kids will love coloring the fun illustrations in this book. Whether they follow the numbered suggestions at the bottom of each page or make their own color choices as they go, each child will bring special sparkle to these lovely drawings. And they'll have fun reading the rhyming captions too.

Sally dresses at the start of the day.
She can hardly wait to play!

Color the pictures like this:

1 = red
2 = light blue
3 = yellow
4 = pink

5 = black
6 = light brown
7 = light yellow green
8 = dark green

9 = navy blue
10 = violet
11 = orange
14 = peach

When you sit each morning at the breakfast table,
Eat foods that make you strong and able.

Color the pictures like this:

1 = red   5 = black   9 = navy blue
2 = light blue   6 = light brown   11 = orange
3 = yellow   7 = light yellow green   12 = dark brown
4 = pink   8 = dark green   13 = gray

Little Peter, like all girls and boys,
Loves to play with colorful toys.

Color the pictures like this:

1 = red	6 = light brown	10 = violet
2 = light blue	7 = light yellow green	12 = dark brown
3 = yellow	8 = dark green	14 = peach
5 = black	9 = navy blue	15 = turquoise

The fluttering butterfly and quick little mouse,
Live in the woods near the house.

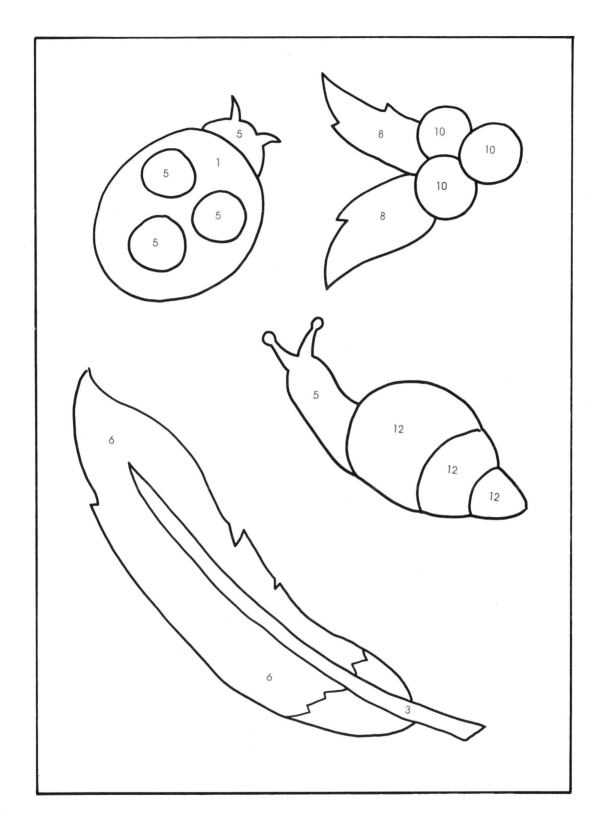

Color the pictures like this:

1 = red   5 = black   10 = violet
2 = light blue   6 = light brown   12 = dark brown
3 = yellow   7 = light yellow green   13 = gray
4 = pink   8 = dark green   15 = turquoise

Annie knows that springtime showers,
Bring the summer, sun, and flowers.

Color the pictures like this:

1 = red   6 = light brown   10 = violet
2 = light blue   7 = light yellow green   11 = orange
3 = yellow   8 = dark green   12 = dark brown
5 = black   9 = navy blue

13

Nancy works in her garden for hours,
Planting, weeding, and watering flowers.

Color the pictures like this:

1 = red

2 = light blue

3 = yellow

4 = pink

6 = light brown

7 = light yellow green

8 = dark green

11 = orange

12 = dark brown

13 = gray

14 = peach

Building sand castles in the sun,
Makes the summer so much fun.

Color the pictures like this:

1 = red
2 = light blue
3 = yellow
5 = black

6 = light brown
7 = light yellow green
8 = dark green
9 = navy blue

13 = gray
14 = peach
15 = turquoise

**Chocolate! Vanilla! Strawberry, too!
In the ice cream truck is a cone for you.**

Color the pictures like this:

1 = red   6 = light brown   11 = orange
2 = light blue   7 = light yellow green   12 = dark brown
3 = yellow   9 = navy blue   13 = gray
4 = pink   10 = violet   14 = peach
5 = black

19

When a new day dawns on the farm,
The rooster crows to sound the alarm.

Color the picture like this:

1 = red   5 = black   9 = navy blue
2 = light blue   6 = light brown   11 = orange
3 = yellow   7 = light yellow green   12 = dark brown
4 = pink   8 = dark green

Don't you wish that you could get,
A cat, a bird, or fish for a pet?

Color the pictures like this:

1 = red   5 = black   9 = navy blue
2 = light blue   6 = light brown   11 = orange
3 = yellow   7 = light yellow green   12 = dark brown
4 = pink   8 = dark green

A bat, a ghost, a pirate, and a queen,
Spook each other on Halloween.

Color the pictures like this:

1 = red   6 = light brown   11 = orange
3 = yellow   8 = dark green   12 = dark brown
4 = pink   9 = navy blue   14 = peach
5 = black   10 = violet   15 = turquoise

Marcy sings "rub-a-dub-dub,"
As she plays with bubbles in the tub.

Color the pictures like this:

1 = red	5 = black	8 = dark green
2 = light blue	6 = light brown	11 = orange
3 = yellow	7 = light yellow green	13 = gray

John is happy when it snows,
He bundles up and out he goes.

Color the pictures like this:

1 = red   5 = black   10 = violet
2 = light blue   6 = light brown   11 = orange
3 = yellow   7 = light yellow green   15 = turquoise

Eleanor paints and glues and measures,
When school is done, she takes home her treasures.

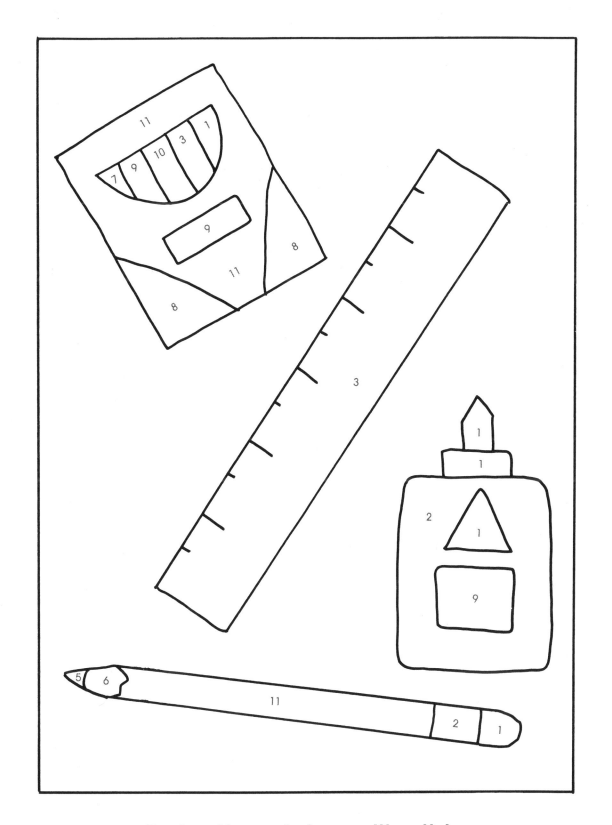

Color the pictures like this:

1 = red	6 = light brown	10 = violet
2 = light blue	7 = light yellow green	11 = orange
3 = yellow	8 = dark green	12 = dark brown
5 = black	9 = navy blue	14 = peach

Baking cookies is delicious fun.
May I eat one when they're done?

Color the picture like this:

1 = red	5 = black	12 = dark brown
2 = light blue	6 = light brown	13 = gray
3 = yellow	9 = navy blue	15 = turquoise